WALT DISNEY'S CLASSIC

Bambi

Based on Walt Disney's
full-length animated classic

Adapted by Jan Carr

SCHOLASTIC INC.
New York Toronto London Auckland Sydney

To OUR SON DAVID

WE HOPE YOU ENJOY THIS STORY

WE LOVE YOU MUCH

MOM & DAD

CHRISTMAS 1989

The edition containing the full text of *BAMBI, A Life in the Woods* by Felix Salten, is published by Simon and Schuster.

Walt Disney's Bambi. Based on the original story by Felix Salten.

ISBN 0-590-41664-2

12 11 10 9 8 7 6 5 4 3   8 9/8 0 1 2 3/9

Printed in the U.S.A.

Bambi

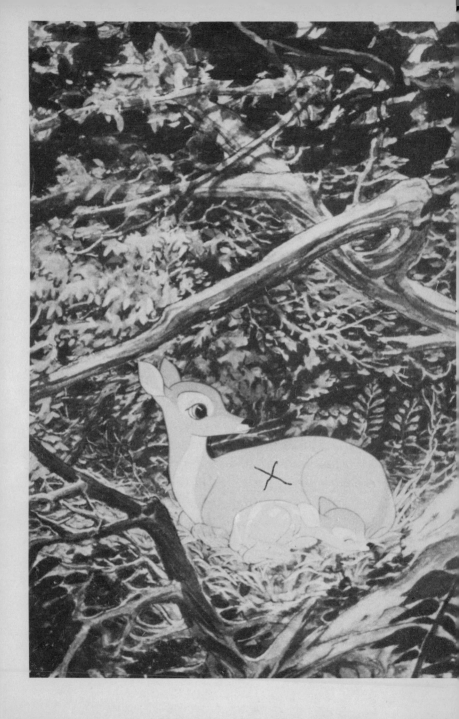

1

It was morning in the deep, green forest. The smell of pine was all around. The forest had many tall trees. It also had clear, sparkling streams and soft, grassy meadows.

Many animals lived in the forest. There was lots of food for them and plenty of places they could find shelter. The forest was untouched, a perfect home for woodland creatures. No people lived there, just animals.

As the sun came up this particular day, it seemed like any other morning. A mother bird fed breakfast to her hungry babies. A little mouse washed his face with the morning dew. And the wise old owl was already asleep for the day and snoring in the hollow of his tree.

However, this wasn't just any morning. News of a great event spread fast. An excited blue jay flew quickly through the forest, chirping loudly. As he passed by, all the animals stopped to listen to his important news. Bunnies hopped from their burrows. Quail left their nests. Soon all the forest animals knew that something had happened in the nearby thicket. They began to hurry there to see for themselves.

One of the animals was a little bunny named Thumper. He stopped in front of the sleeping owl and loudly thumped his foot on the ground.

"Wake up!" he cried.

The owl blinked his eyes.

"Oh, what now?" he said sleepily.

"Wake up, Friend Owl," said Thumper.

The owl looked around at all the animals hurrying by.

"Hey! What's going on around here?" he asked.

"It's happened! It's happened!" said another bunny.

"The new prince is born!" said Thumper. "We're going to see him. Come on! You'd better hurry up!"

Thumper took off. He wanted to get to the thicket quickly. The owl flew right behind.

2

At the thicket, all the animals were gathered in a circle.

"Ahhh," they sighed. "My, my."

Before them lay a mother deer. Beside her was the attraction — a beautiful newborn fawn, sleeping soundly. His fur was a rich shade of brown, and it was speckled with soft white spots.

The owl flew up into a tree and looked down proudly.

"Well," he said. "This is quite an occasion!"

A mother quail and her babies ran in to join the circle of admirers.

"Yes, sir," said the owl. "It isn't every day a prince is born. You're to be congratulated," he said to the mother deer.

"Thank you very much," she said. The mother looked at her little fawn and nudged him gently.

"Come on. Wake up," she said softly. "We have company."

The little fawn opened his eyes and looked

around. There were so many other animals there, staring at him!

"Hello. Hello there, little prince," said the animals.

The owl looked down from his branch.

"Yoo hoo," he cried. "Yoo hoooo!"

The fawn jumped at the sound. He huddled closer to his mother. But when the owl smiled at him, the fawn smiled shyly back. Then he braced himself to try to stand.

"Look!" shouted Thumper. "He's trying to get up."

The fawn stood up. His young legs were shaking.

"Kind of wobbly, isn't he?" said Thumper.

"Thumper!" cried his mother.

"Well, he is," said Thumper. He hopped right up to the fawn. "Aren't you?" he said.

The fawn fell backward beside his mother and then opened his mouth in a wide yawn.

"Looks to me like he's getting kinda sleepy," said the owl. "I think it's time we all left. Come on," he said to the other animals. "Shoo! Shoo!"

At his command all the birds flew from their perches, and the animals scattered.

The mother rabbit gathered her children together. She had all of them — all except Thumper, that is. Thumper was still sitting right by the fawn. When the fawn yawned again, Thumper stuck his head right in the fawn's mouth to look inside.

"Thumper!" called the mother rabbit. "Come on!"

Thumper hopped over to the fawn's mother.

"What are you going to call him?" he asked her.

"Well," said the mother deer, "I think I'll call him Bambi."

"Bambi," said Thumper. "Yep. I guess that'll do all right."

Thumper hopped off to join his own family.

"Bambi," said the mother deer. She nuzzled the sweet, sleeping fawn. "My little Bambi."

In the thicket, Bambi slept at his mother's side. He was safe and loved. On a nearby rock stood a tall, proud stag. He looked protectively toward the thicket and beyond, across the forest.

3

Not long after that, Bambi began to walk. His legs grew stronger. His mother decided to take him for his first long walk through the forest.

All the forest animals were still very interested in the young prince. When Bambi walked by, the squirrels looked up from their acorns.

"Walking already!" said one. "Well, what do you know!"

Mrs. Quail was taking a walk, too. Her babies followed behind her in a line.

"Good morning," Mrs. Quail called to Bambi's mother. "And where's the young prince this morning?"

Bambi toddled out from behind some trees.

"Ohhh!" said Mrs. Quail in surprise.

All the little quail hopped up and down.

"Good morning, Young Prince," they twittered.

Bambi met many new friends that morning. He saw a mole family furrow through the ground.

How did they do that? Where did they go? He passed a birch tree and saw a family of opossums hanging upside down from a branch. Bambi looked up at the funny opossums and scampered away. It was fun to take walks. It was fun to be so free.

4

Bambi romped through the forest, but soon his legs began to tire. He was still rather new to this walking business. His legs started to wobble. He slipped and fell flat on the ground.

As it happened, the rabbit family was hopping by.

"What's the matter?" asked one of the bunnies. "Did the young prince fall down?"

"Is he hurt?" asked Thumper.

Bambi's mother went to his side.

"No," she said. "He's all right."

Bambi lay helpless, sprawled on the ground. Thumper looked at him and shook his head.

"He doesn't walk very good, does he?" said Thumper.

"Thumper!" yelled his mother. She folded her arms and looked sternly at her son. "What did your father tell you this morning?"

Thumper looked off guiltily. He squirmed.

"Uh," said Thumper. "Uh, well." He repeated

11

the lesson his father had taught. "If you can't say anything nice, don't say nothing at all," he said.

Bambi's mother nudged her fawn to get up.

"Come on," she said. "Try again."

All the rabbits ran to Bambi to give him encouragement.

"Come on," said Thumper. "Get up!"

Bambi stuck his tail in the air and pulled himself back on his feet. All the bunnies giggled. Bambi scampered off again and his new friends hopped along.

Bambi and the bunnies ran through the forest. Thumper stopped at a big tree trunk that had fallen to the ground. It was hollow. Thumper thumped his foot in excitement.

"I'm thumpin'!" he cried. "That's why they call me Thumper!"

An echo bounced out from the hollow.

"That's why they call me Thumper!" it repeated.

Thumper looked up in surprise.

"Thumper!" cried Thumper again.

"Thumper!" came the echo.

Thumper ran through the log. Bambi and the others followed.

Farther on through the woods a very large tree had fallen and blocked the animals' path. All the rabbits hopped easily over it. Bambi ran up to it and stopped still, blinking his eyes.

"Come on!" called Thumper. "You can do it."

Thumper hopped over the tree again, to show Bambi how.

"Like this!" he said.

Bambi backed away from the tree to get a running start. He wiggled his tail. He leaped forward. Bambi didn't quite clear the tree. He landed right on top, his legs sprawled out on either side.

5

Y ou didn't hop far enough!" said Thumper.
Bambi looked behind at his back legs and
pulled one of them over the log.

"That's it!" said Thumper. "Now the other one."

Bambi smiled. This was easy. He pulled the
other leg over and stood up. Bambi, Thumper,
and the other bunnies ran off through the woods.

It was a clear, sunny day. As Bambi and his
friends scampered about, birds flew overhead,
singing happily. Bambi stopped to listen.

"Those are birds," Thumper told Bambi.

Bambi blinked his eyes.

"Burrr," he said.

Thumper looked at him in surprise.

"Look! He's trying to talk!" cried Thumper.

"He's trying to say *bird!*" said another of the
bunnies.

Thumper hopped close to Bambi.

"Say *bird!*" said Thumper.

"Burr," said Bambi.

17

"Bur-*duh!*" said Thumper.

"Burr," said Bambi.

Thumper shook his head. "No," he said. "Bur-*duh!*"

All the rabbits gathered around.

"Bur-*duh!*" said Bambi. He said it! Bambi let out a big, triumphant sigh. The bunnies went scampering to Mrs. Rabbit, who stood talking with Bambi's mother.

"He talked! He talked! He talked, Mama!" they cried all at once. "The young prince said *bird!*"

"Bird! Bird! Bird!" Bambi said over and over. He danced around, proudly chanting his new word.

A butterfly landed on his tail. Bambi looked at it and smiled.

"Bird!" said Bambi.

"No," said Thumper. "That's not a bird. That's a butterfly."

"Butterfly?" asked Bambi.

Thumper nodded.

Bambi looked back at his tail, but the butterfly had flown off. Bambi looked around for it, confused, then bounded off to a patch of brightly colored flowers.

"Butterfly!" he said, looking down at the flowers.

"No," said Thumper, close behind. "That's a flower."

"Flower," said Bambi.

"Uh-huh," said Thumper. "It's pretty."

"Pretty," said Bambi.

Bambi leaned down to sniff the flowers. Suddenly another creature rose out of the flowers, right in front of Bambi's nose. It was a skunk, face to face with Bambi. Bambi was delighted.

"Flower!" he cried.

Thumper fell on the ground, laughing.

"No, no, no!" he said. "That's not a flower. He's a little. . . ."

The little skunk spoke up.

"Oh, that's all right," he said shyly. "He can call me Flower if he wants to. I don't mind."

Bambi and the skunk smiled at each other.

"Pretty, pretty flower," said Bambi.

"Oh, gosh," blushed the skunk.

Thumper giggled. The skunk giggled, too.

6

Bambi, Thumper, and Flower played together for hours. They didn't notice the sky growing darker. They didn't notice the black clouds rolling in front of the sun.

Suddenly raindrops started to fall. Bambi and Thumper raced back through the forest.

In the sky, above the trees, a bolt of lightning flashed. Thunder boomed. The two animals looked up in fright.

"I think I'd better go home now," said Thumper.

He ran off through the woods, leaving Bambi behind. Another loud clap of thunder rumbled through the trees. Bambi ran to find his mother. Mother deer and baby ran back to their thicket.

The thicket kept Bambi almost dry. He lay underneath a spray of branches and watched big drops of rain roll down the leaves past his nose.

All around them, other animals were also taking shelter. A mother bird covered her babies with her wing. A little mouse scampered under a toadstool. Only the ducks stayed out in the rain, paddling across the pond.

Bambi laid his head down beside his mother. His eyelids drooped. He was tired. Maybe he would drift to sleep to the lulling patter of the rain.

Just then, more lightning flashed across the sky. Bambi jumped up. He pranced around, nervous, scared. Thunder crackled. Bambi ran to his mother and tucked himself against her warm side. He stayed there, wide-eyed, through the long electric storm.

Finally the rain slowed and stopped. The sky cleared. The animals of the forest crept out of their holes and looked around.

In the thicket, though, Bambi was still. He had finally fallen asleep. Bambi's mother nuzzled his young, sleeping face. Around them, the rain-soaked forest dried slowly in the warming sun.

7

The months passed. Little by little, Bambi was growing. There were still many places he hadn't seen, though, and still many things he didn't know. Bambi's mother knew it was time to teach him.

One morning, in the forest, Bambi was eating his breakfast grass.

"What are we going to do today, Mother?" he asked.

"I'm going to take you to the meadow," said his mother.

"Meadow?" asked Bambi. "What's the meadow?"

"It's a very wonderful place," she said.

"Then why haven't we been there before?" asked Bambi.

"You weren't big enough," said his mother.

It was a long walk to the meadow. Bambi scampered through the forest, and his mother walked steadily ahead. Bambi caught up with her.

"Mother, you know what?" he said. "We're not the only deer in the forest."

"Where did you hear that?" asked his mother.

"Thumper told me," said Bambi.

"Well, he's right," said his mother. "There are many deer in the forest besides us. You'll see them sometime."

"In the meadow?" asked Bambi.

"Perhaps," said his mother. She stopped and looked around. "Hush now! We're almost there."

Bambi and his mother stood at the edge of the forest. Just beyond the trees there was a large, open area. It was full of soft grass.

"The meadow!" shouted Bambi. He bounded out of the woods.

"Wait!" cried his mother. She raced in front of Bambi and blocked his path. "Bambi," she said sternly, "you must *never* rush into the meadow."

Bambi looked up at her, frightened.

"There might be danger," she explained. "Out there we are unprotected. The meadow is wide and open, and there are no trees or bushes to hide us, so we have to be very careful. Wait here," she added. "I'll go out first and see if it's safe."

Bambi's mother crept out of the bushes and into the open field. She peered about. She sniffed the air. The meadow seemed to be safe.

"Come on, Bambi," she called. "It's all right."

Bambi leaped out into the open. All this space to run! All this grass to eat! Bambi had never imagined a place so wonderful. He ran this way and that. Fast, faster. He bounded across the meadow in swift, graceful leaps.

"Good morning, Prince Bambi," came a voice. "Good morning, Young Prince," called another.

It was the rabbit family. They, too, had come to the meadow. The bunnies were sitting in a patch of weeds, eating wildflowers.

"What are you eating?" asked Bambi.

"Clover," said Thumper. "It's delicious. Why don't you try some?"

Bambi lowered his head into the patch and bit off a clump of greens.

"No, no!" said Thumper. "Not that green stuff!"

Thumper plucked the juicy sweet flower off one of the clover plants and popped it into his mouth to show Bambi.

"Thumper!" cried his mother. Thumper was in trouble again. "What did your father tell you?"

"About what?" asked Thumper, as innocently as he could.

"About eating the blossoms and leaving the greens," said his mother.

"Oh, that," said Thumper. Thumper cleared his throat to recite his father's lesson.

> "Eating greens
> is a special treat.
> It makes long ears
> and great big feet!"

Thumper leaned close to Bambi's ear and whispered,

> "But it sure is
> awful stuff to eat!"

The last part, of course, Thumper had made up himself.

8

There were many new and interesting things to discover in the meadow. A frog hopped out of the weeds and leaped to a nearby pond. Bambi followed. He looked at his reflection in the smooth surface of the water.

Suddenly there were two faces reflected in the pond! Bambi whirled around. Beside him stood another fawn. It was a little girl fawn. She smiled at him. Bambi jumped back in fright and scrambled up the hill to his mother.

Bambi scurried under his mother and hid behind her legs. The girl fawn chased behind.

"That's little Faline," said Bambi's mother. She was standing with another doe, Faline's mother.

Faline wagged her tail.

"He's kind of bashful, isn't he, Mama?" Faline asked.

"Well," said her mother. "Maybe he wouldn't be if you'd say hello."

Faline jumped right up to Bambi.

"Hello, Bambi!" she said.

Bambi backed away shyly.

"Aren't you going to answer her?" his mother asked him.

Bambi wrinkled his nose.

"You're not afraid, are you?" she asked.

Afraid? Bambi shook his head.

"Well, then," said his mother. "Go on. Say hello."

"Hello," said Bambi in a very small voice.

Faline giggled. She ran off, laughing. Bambi ran after her.

When they reached the pond, Faline jumped at Bambi, waving her front hooves. Bambi fell backward into the water. Faline giggled again. She stuck her head through the reeds and licked Bambi's face.

"Yeeowww!" Bambi cried. He jumped to his feet and butted against her. This time, Faline fell. The two chased each other across the meadow to a large rock.

A herd of big male deer was very close to where the two fawns were playing. Each one had great, branching antlers. Faline ran off, still playing. Bambi stayed on the rock, watching the stags.

Some of the stags were fighting. They locked their antlers and pushed each other fiercely. Other stags ran through the meadow, leaping off rocks.

Suddenly, as Bambi watched, all the stags turned and ran in the same direction. Then they stopped and formed a line. They stood at attention and looked to the forest. Bambi looked, too.

Out of the forest walked another stag. This one was strikingly handsome, and he was larger than all the rest. He walked slowly and proudly through the trees and into the meadow. When he passed Bambi, he stopped for a very long moment and looked at the young, gaping fawn.

9

Bambi ran to his mother.

"He stopped and looked at me," said Bambi, panting.

"Yes, I know," said his mother. Was she smiling? Bambi couldn't tell.

Bambi looked back toward the great stag.

"Why was everyone still when he came to the meadow?" Bambi asked.

"Everyone respects him," said his mother, "for of all the deer in the forest, not one has lived half so long." She, too, looked back across the meadow. "He's very brave," she said, "and very wise. That's why he's known as the Great Prince of the Forest."

The stag surveyed the meadow and walked back into the woods. He climbed a tall rock and scanned the land all around. In the sky above him, some birds flew by. They were chirping loudly. The stag could tell that they were fleeing something. He bounded off the rock and dashed back to the meadow.

In the meadow many deer were standing around, grazing. When they saw the stag race among them, they knew there must be danger near. They, too, took off, running into the safety of the forest.

"Faline!" Faline's mother called through the scrambling animals. Faline ran to her side. The two dashed off.

"Bambi!" Bambi's mother called his name, but Bambi was lost, caught in the sudden stampede. Animals were running everywhere. Bambi dashed wildly among them.

"Mother!" he called. He could not find her. "Mother!"

Suddenly there was the stag. He was at Bambi's side, looking down at him. The stag leaped away and Bambi followed on his heels. The two deer fled into the forest. Bambi's mother ran, too. Behind them, loud gunshots rang through the forest. The deer leaped into the thicket, where they could not be seen. They stayed there, hiding, wide-eyed and alert, until the danger had passed.

At last, Bambi's mother crept out from her cover. She looked around.

"Come on out, Bambi," she said.

Bambi stayed in the thicket. His heart was still pounding.

"Come on," said his mother. "It's safe now.

We don't have to hide any longer."

Bambi stuck his head out of the brush and looked at his mother.

"What happened?" he asked. "Why did we all run?"

"Man was in the forest," said his mother.

That's all she said, but her voice was grave. Bambi knew he had learned something important.

Bambi's mother stretched her cramped neck and moved off slowly through the woods. Bambi caught up and trotted right behind her.

10

Summer gave way to fall, and fall passed into winter. A sharp chill now hung in the air. The last leaves fell from the trees.

One night, while Bambi was asleep, a heavy snow fell and covered the forest. In the morning, when he awoke, nothing looked the same. Bambi stared out from the thicket.

"What's all that white stuff?" he asked his mother.

"Why, that's snow," she smiled. "Winter has come."

Bambi touched his hoof to the soft, cold whiteness. It left a mark. He pranced out into the snow and looked behind him. His hooves had left a long trail of tracks! Bambi ran ahead and fell into a big mound of snow.

Thumper was also out for a morning's play.

"Hiya, Bambi," he called to his friend.

Bambi shook the snow off his head and ran after Thumper.

"Watch what I can do!" Thumper yelled. He got a running start and slid across the snow. He slid onto the pond, which was frozen over with ice.

"Come on! It's all right!" he yelled. "Look! The water's stiff!"

"Yippee!" yelled Bambi.

When Bambi ran out to the pond, his legs were not as steady as Thumper's. He slipped and landed on his belly. When he tried to get up, his legs again slid out from under him. Thumper got behind him and pushed him back to the opposite bank.

"Kind of wobbly, aren't you?" Thumper said.

Bambi would have tried the ice again, but suddenly he heard a strange loud sound. Bambi looked at Thumper. The two went to explore.

The sound was coming from a cave. They peered in. Inside the cave was Flower the skunk. He was sound asleep, and snoring loudly.

"Wake up! Wake up!" called Thumper. He thumped his leg near Flower's ear. Flower woke up groggily.

"Is it spring yet?" Flower asked, blinking his eyes.

"Nope," said Bambi. "Winter's just started."

"What are you doing? Hibernating?" asked Thumper.

Flower yawned and smacked his lips.

"Uh-huh," he said.

"What do you want to do that for?" Bambi asked.
Flower smiled a sleepy smile.

"All of us flowers sleep in the winter," he laughed. With that, his eyes slipped closed, and he snuggled back into a warm ball. "Well," he said. "Goodnight."

All that winter, the forest stayed covered with snow. The animals that liked to hibernate stayed snug in their beds. The others, like Bambi, foraged the cold woods for food. There wasn't much to be found, though. Nothing was growing. There was plenty of snow but little to eat.

Bambi's mother taught him to reach up and eat the bark that covered the trees. That was something, but not enough. By the end of the winter, there was not even much bark left.

"Winter sure is long, isn't it?" Bambi said to his mother.

"It seems long," she said, "but it won't last forever."

Bambi lay beside his mother and snuggled against her to block out the winter wind.

"I'm awfully hungry, Mother," said Bambi.

"Yes, I know," she said.

11

The winter wore on. It seemed as if spring would never come. Then, one morning, when Bambi's mother was looking for food, she spotted a patch of young, green grass. It was peeping out from under the snow.

"Bambi!" she called. "Come here! Look! New spring grass!"

Bambi ate hungrily from the patch, and his mother did, too. It had been a long time since they had tasted anything so good.

"Now that spring is here," thought Bambi, "life will again be free and easy."

Suddenly Bambi's mother looked up, startled. She pricked her ears. She glanced quickly about, this way and that.

"Quick!" she said. "The thicket!"

Bambi took off running and his mother ran behind him. Bambi jumped across a stream. He tore through the snow.

"Faster, Bambi!" called his mother. "Don't look back! Keep running!"

A loud boom echoed through the forest. Bambi recognized the sound. He had heard it before. It was a gunshot.

Bambi ran through the forest to the safety of the thicket.

"We made it!" he panted. "We made it, Mother!"

Bambi looked around. His mother was not there. Hadn't she been running right behind him?

Bambi ran out of the thicket.

"Mother!" he cried. "Mother!"

He looked around. Where was she? Bambi was frantic. He called and called his mother's name, but no one answered. Bambi's mother was gone. Bambi was alone in the forest. His eyes welled up with tears.

Another animal moved silently through the trees. It was the great stag. He had seen what had happened. He came to Bambi's side.

"Your mother can't be with you anymore," he said.

Bambi looked up at him sadly.

"Man has taken her away. Now you must be brave," said the stag, "and learn to walk alone."

Bambi's tears ran down his nose.

"Come, my son," the stag said gently.

The stag moved slowly through the cold, quiet forest. Bambi followed his father home.

12

Spring. Trees blossomed. Flowers bloomed. The forest was full of bright colors and sweet smells. The songs of birds filled the air.

The warming sun had brought many birds back to the forest. Suddenly birds were everywhere, flying, singing. They chirped and twittered. They kissed and nuzzled. This was spring, after all.

On this spring morning the owl was in the hollow of his tree. He was trying to sleep. The singing woke him up. He looked around grumpily.

"Hey! Hey! Stop that racket!" he shouted. "Scat! Shoo!"

The owl jumped up and flapped his wings.

"Woo! Woo!" he shouted.

Birds scattered from all the nearby trees and flew off through the forest.

"There!" said the owl. "I guess that'll teach them."

The owl was pleased with himself and ready to

go back to sleep. Above him, two new birds fluttered about.

"Tweet, tweet," they chirped happily.

"Oh, what's the use?" said the owl. He flew off in disgust to find himself another tree.

"Same thing every year," he grumbled. "Tweet, tweet, tweet. Tweet, tweet, tweet. Love's sweet song." He crinkled up his face angrily. "Pain in the pin feathers, I'd call it."

The owl settled onto a branch and folded his wings across his chest. Finally. Maybe now he could actually get some sleep.

As he closed his eyes, the branches began to shake. The whole tree was shaking! The owl clutched onto his perch tightly. What was going on?

13

At the foot of the tree was a young stag. He had grown new spring antlers and was rubbing them hard against the tree trunk to sharpen them.

"Stop it!" the owl called down. "Get out of here!"

The young stag raised his head. It was Bambi.

"Hello, Friend Owl," he said. "Don't you remember me?"

"Bambi!" said the owl. "Well, if it isn't the young prince! My, my, how you've changed. Turn around. Let me look at you."

Bambi held his head and antlers high. He turned them this way and that for the owl to see.

"I see you've traded in your spots for a pair of antlers," said the owl. He chuckled at the sight of the grown-up deer. "You know," he said, "just the other day I was talking to myself about you, and we were wondering what became of you."

Bambi laughed.

"Hello, Bambi," came another voice. A rabbit

hopped up. He thumped his hind foot rapidly on the ground.

"Remember me?" he asked.

"Thumper!" said Bambi.

"Righto!" said his friend.

From the corner of his eye Bambi noticed a fluffy black-and-white tail rising from a small patch of flowers. It was a skunk. He stuck his head up.

"Hi, fellows!" he said.

"Flower!" said Bambi.

The three friends were together once again. Two birds flew over their heads, twittering loudly. Two more flew by, then another pair.

"What's the matter with them?" asked Flower.

"Why are they acting that way?" asked Thumper.

"Why, don't you know?" asked the owl. "They're twitter-pated!"

Bambi looked at Thumper. Thumper looked at Flower.

"Twitter-pated?" the three said together.

"Yes," said the owl. "Nearly everybody gets twitter-pated in the springtime."

Bambi, Thumper, and Flower looked at him. What was he talking about?

"For example," said the owl. "You're walking along, minding your own business, then all of a sudden, you run smack into a pretty face. Woo! Woo!" he yelled.

Flower jumped.

"You begin to get weak in the knees," said the owl. "Your head's in a whirl. And then you feel light as a feather. You're walking on air. And then, you know what? You completely lose your head!"

"Gosh!" said Thumper.

"Gee whiz!" said Flower.

"Terrible!" said Bambi.

"And that ain't all!" said the owl. "It can happen to anybody. It can happen to you! And you! And even you!" he said, pointing right at Flower. "So you'd better be careful!"

"Well, it's not gonna happen to me!" said Thumper.

"Me, neither!" said Bambi.

Flower shook his head from side to side.

"Me, neither!" he said.

The three friends marched proudly off through the forest. None of them were quite sure what the owl was talking about, but whatever it was, it didn't sound good.

14

Bambi romped through the forest, with Thumper and Flower following. The three friends had not gone very far when Flower stopped short. He noticed something odd, a patch of flowers that seemed to be shaking and giggling. When he walked up to the blossoms, a head popped out.

It was a girl skunk, a very pretty girl skunk. She smiled at Flower. Flower liked the way her eyes twinkled. He felt himself leaning toward her. His nose brushed hers. Flower jumped back in surprise. What was he doing? He ran back from the girl and stared at her.

The girl skunk was not only pretty, she was also a very good flirt. She smiled at Flower. She waved her paw at him. She was very cute and very coy. Flower waved back.

Before he knew it, he was kissing her. A thrill ran through his body. So this was love!

By this time, Bambi and Thumper had noticed that their friend was no longer behind them. They

turned around to look for him. They saw him running off through the flowers, and they saw he was chasing after the girl skunk.

"Flower!" yelled Bambi.

Flower stopped only long enough to shrug his shoulders sheepishly. What could he do? He ran off after his new girlfriend.

"Huh!" said Thumper. He shook his head, disgusted. "Twitter-pated!"

Bambi and Thumper turned and walked off. There were only the two of them left now.

Not far down the trail, there was another little animal. It was a bunny, a girl bunny. She was licking the flowers.

"Ohhhh!" she said, when she saw Thumper pass. She liked Thumper. He looked awfully cute.

When Thumper saw the girl bunny, he liked her, too. His mouth fell open. His ears began to twitch.

The girl hummed a little song and sidled up beside Thumper.

"Hello," she said. Then she leaned right over and kissed him. What was she doing? Thumper's hind leg thumped the ground rapidly.

When Bambi looked back, Thumper was lying on the ground. His head was in the girl bunny's lap. She was stroking his ear and singing her honey-eyed, twitter-pated song.

15

Bambi was on his own now. He'd lost not one, but two, friends to twitter-pa —

"Hmm," Bambi thought, "*what* was it called? Twitter-pation? Twitter-potato?"

Well, whatever it was, Bambi couldn't be bothered. He waded into the stream and took a drink.

"Hello, Bambi," said a voice.

Bambi looked up. There beside him stood a deer, a female deer.

"Don't you remember me?" she asked. She smiled. "I'm Faline."

Bambi gulped and started to back away from her. *This* was Faline? Why, she was grown-up. She was so. . . . Well, she was. . . . Faline was a *doe*, and such a pretty one, too.

Bambi backed into a tree. His antlers got caught in the branches. Faline laughed and licked Bambi's face. Bambi tore his antlers free and then let out a long, happy sigh. This girl business wasn't so bad after all, Bambi thought. In fact, it was heavenly. It was like floating on air. Was Bambi's head really in the clouds or did it just feel that way?

Bambi was not the only young stag in the forest, though. Another stag also had his eye on Faline, and when he saw Faline lick Bambi, he was jealous.

Before Bambi knew what was happening, the other stag ran up to him, butted him, and knocked him down.

Bambi got up, surprised. He had certainly never expected anything like this.

The other stag pushed Faline into the woods. He wanted her for himself.

"Bambi!" Faline cried, frightened. "Bambi!"

Bambi had never fought before, but this made him angry! How could that stag knock him down and then push Faline around?

Bambi pawed the ground and snorted. He ran after the stag, his head and antlers down. He was ready to fight.

The other stag was a skilled fighter. When they locked antlers, he tossed Bambi to the ground. When Bambi came after him, the stag rose up on his hind legs and kicked his front hooves at Bambi. Bambi didn't give up. The stag leaped at him. Bambi jumped out of reach.

It was a long, hard fight. The two stags locked antlers. Both were strong. Both were determined.

Finally, in a moment of great strength, Bambi swung his head. He threw the other stag over a cliff and into the water below.

Bambi had won! The fight was over! Faline kissed his neck. This time, Bambi kissed her back.

16

From that day on, Bambi and Faline spent all
their time together. They were quite happy.
They had each other, and they had the rich, boun-
tiful forest that was their home. Bambi and Faline
played in the meadow. They romped through the
streams. They chased each other through the
sparkling waterfall. It was a very good time.

Early one morning, though, Bambi awoke with
a start. He knew something was wrong. Faline
was still asleep beside him in the thicket. Bambi
got up quietly to look around.

He walked through the forest. Nothing was different that he could see. He climbed up a hill. No,
nothing different. He walked to the edge of the
cliff and looked down. There, in the clearing, was
smoke. It was coming from a campfire.

"It's Man," said a voice.

Bambi looked up. Beside him stood his father,
the great stag. The stag saw the campfire, too.

"Man is here again," he said, "and there are

many this time. We must go deep into the forest."

Many of the other forest animals had already sensed the danger. Birds were flying away from the clearing and squawking loudly.

"Hurry!" said the stag. "Follow me!"

The stag took off running, and Bambi almost followed. Then he remembered.

"Faline!" he cried out. He ran back into the forest to save his truest friend.

17

In the thicket, Faline was still asleep. The sound of the birds awoke her. They were frightened and calling wildly. Faline pricked up her ears. Danger! She looked beside her. Bambi was gone.

"Bambi!" Faline cried out. "Bambi, where are you?"

Faline ran into the woods to find him. Bambi ran back to the thicket. But by the time he got there, Faline was gone.

"Faline!" Bambi called. "Faline!"

All the small animals in the forest were now frightened and alert. Some ducked inside tree hollows for safety. A group of pheasants scrambled to hide in a patch of tall weeds. All the pheasants were scared, but one, the youngest one, was terrified.

"Listen!" cried the frightened one. "He's coming!"

"Hush!" whispered his friends. "Be quiet!"

"He's coming closer!" cried the pheasant.

"Shh! Don't get excited," said his friends.

The poor little pheasant paced nervously in the weeds.

"We'd better fly," he said.

"No!" said his friends, trying to calm him. "Don't fly. Whatever you do, don't fly."

But the poor little pheasant was too scared to listen.

"I can't stand it any longer!" he shouted. He flapped his wings and flew into the air above the weeds.

Moments later the sound of gunshot rang through the air, and the poor pheasant fell to the ground. He'd been shot by hunters.

More gunshots sounded. Terror shot through all the animals. Faline ran through the forest in a frenzy. Bambi raced about, looking for her.

"Faline!" he called.

A bullet hit the ground close to Bambi. Everywhere, feathers fell. More birds had been shot.

By this time, Faline had reached the cliffs. She stopped. Behind her she heard a sound. It was a different sound, but just as frightening. Dogs!

Faline kept her wits about her. She scrambled across a rock. A pack of hounds was close behind. The dogs were on her trail.

Faline dashed through the rocks. She could hear the dogs gaining. They were almost at her heels.

Panic raced through Faline's veins. The dogs barked angrily.

One of the dogs jumped at Faline. She leaped into the air and onto the tallest of the rocks. She stood there, pinned against the face of the stone. Below her all the dogs barked furiously. They jumped up, snapping and snarling.

"Bambi!" Faline cried.

18

From across the forest, Bambi heard Faline's cry. He raced to the cliffs and was just in time. The pack was jumping at Faline. Bambi lowered his antlers, leaped at the dogs, and sent them running.

The fight was not yet over, though. It had just begun. Bambi had surprised the dogs, but they were trained hunters. They growled and charged at him. Bambi fought them back as best he could. He tossed some dogs away with his antlers. Others he kicked. Still others he butted.

"Quick, Faline," he yelled up at his friend. "Jump!"

While Bambi kept the hounds at bay, Faline leaped off the rock and ran from the canyon. When he was sure she was safe, Bambi followed. He scrambled up the rocks, and the dogs chased after him. When Bambi reached the top, he kicked some large, heavy boulders free and let them tumble down behind him. The boulders pushed the dogs back. Together, dogs and rocks skidded and tumbled down the cliff. The rocks pinned the dogs in a heap at the bottom.

Bambi raced off through the forest. He reached a ravine. He leaped to cross it. Just as his long, swift legs stretched to touch the opposite bank, a shot rang out. Bambi stiffened and crumpled to the ground. The hunters had tracked him. They'd shot at him! A bullet had hit Bambi!

Bambi struggled to get to his feet. He was bleeding and in pain. He was weakening quickly. Bambi's legs would not hold him. He fell back. It was no use. He did not have the strength to run.

19

That afternoon was a very dark one in the forest. Bambi was not the only casualty. In another part of the woods an even greater disaster took place. The hunters had left their campfire unattended. The logs had sparked, and the sparks had landed on some crisp, dry twigs that lay on the forest floor. The twigs had, of course, caught fire. Quickly the fire spread to the surrounding bushes and trees. Soon the whole woods were aflame. Man had caused a forest fire.

The wind was high and the fire spread quickly. Small animals darted out of their homes and into the thick smoke. Where should they run? How could they hide?

Bambi smelled the smoke, too. He lifted his head. The fire was near, very near. Bambi knew he should run, but he was too weak.

"Get up, Bambi," said a voice.

It was his father, the great stag.

"You *must* get up," he commanded.

Bambi struggled to his feet. He felt light-headed and his legs shook. Flames licked into the trees around him.

"Now, come with me," said the stag.

The stag led Bambi through the flaming forest. It was hard to know where to run. The fire crackled everywhere. Nothing looked the same.

Water! The stag ran to the stream. He and Bambi walked into the water, following its path. Flaming branches fell from trees behind them. The stag and Bambi pushed on. The stream led them to the top of a waterfall. Water cascaded down the rocks in a steep drop. The stag and Bambi had no choice. Behind them burned the fire. They leaped over the falls and into the cool water below.

Many hours later the fire finally burned itself out. The stag, Bambi, and other forest animals waded out of the stream and stood on its banks. Faline was there, too. She looked around. She twitched her nose. She caught a familiar scent.

"Bambi!" she called.

Bambi ran to Faline and nuzzled his nose in her neck. Both had been saved. They still had each other.

The forest, though, was not the same. It was no longer green and full. It was smoky and charred. It would take a long time for nature to heal this wound.

20

All things pass. The forest animals made their homes again as best they could. Their lives returned to normal.

One morning, as usual, Friend Owl had settled into his hollow to sleep. He was snoozing and snoring. Thumper hopped by — Thumper and four baby bunnies. Thumper was a father now!

"Wake up! Wake up, Friend Owl!" cried Thumper.

"Oh, what now?" said the owl, opening his eyes.

Around him, many of the small forest animals were chattering and scampering. The forest was full of a happy excitement. The animals were all headed in one direction.

The owl blinked his eyes. Something about this seemed very familiar.

"Hey," said the owl. "What's going on here?"

Flower ran past. He, too, was now a father. He had his own new baby skunk with him.

"It's happened!" said Flower. "In the thicket!"

Flower ran off with the other animals and the owl followed. When they got to the thicket, all the animals gathered around.

"Look!" said a raccoon.

Under the brush was Faline, and beside her lay two tiny newborn fawns.

"Two of them!" said the raccoon.

The fawns were light brown and spotted, just as their father had been. One nibbled the other's ear. Both had skinny, wobbly legs.

"Well, sir," said the owl. "I don't believe I've ever seen a more likely pair of fawns. Prince Bambi ought to be mighty proud!"

From a nearby hill, Bambi looked down at the thicket. He *was* proud, very proud. He was proud of his family and of all his woodland neighbors. He was grateful for his wooded home. Bambi looked across the land. Now, he was Prince of the Forest. Like his father, Bambi had grown to be a great, wise stag.